story telling MATH

Look, Grandma!
Ni, Elisi!

Art Coulson

Illustrated by **Madelyn Goodnight**

Charlesbridge

"Look at this!" Bo said, holding up a heavy stone marble. "It's a redbird!"

"Osdadv. That's a nice one, chooch," said Uncle Ben.

They had been working on the marbles for months, getting ready for the Cherokee National Holiday. Every year their family sold crafts in a booth at the festival.

"Those marbles turned out really nice," Uncle Ben said.

"How would you like to help sell them in the booth tomorrow?"

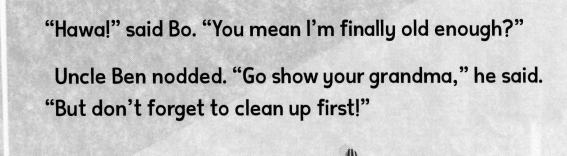

"Hawa!" said Bo. "You mean I'm finally old enough?"

Uncle Ben nodded. "Go show your grandma," he said.
"But don't forget to clean up first!"

Bo carried the marbles out to the porch,
where his grandmother was weaving a basket.

"Ni, Elisi! Look!" he said.

"Gado usdi?" Grandma looked up. "What is it?"

"Uncle Ben says I can help sell the marbles in our booth," he said, "but I need a way to show them off. Can you help me?"

"I need to finish this basket first," said Grandma. "But I'm sure you can find a better container if you look around. Just don't make a big ol' mess!"

Bo ran into the craft room.
The marbles would look great in that pot.

He tried it.

But they didn't all fit.

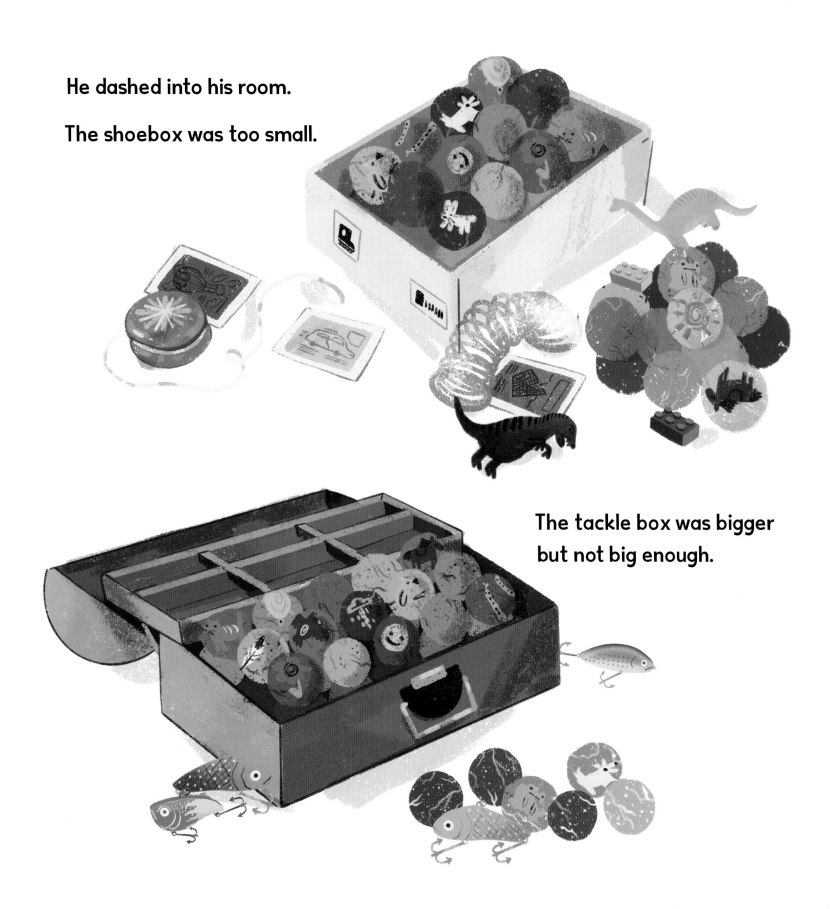

He dashed into his room.

The shoebox was too small.

The tackle box was bigger but not big enough.

What about the wooden tray?

Perfect fit! Bo carried the tray out to the porch.
"Ni, Elisi!" he said. "Won't this look good in our booth?"

His grandmother looked up and frowned.
"Tla. That's way too big," she said.

She handed him a woven mat. "Our booth is small. Your container needs to fit on this mat."

Gado usdi? How could a container take up less space on the table but still hold all the marbles?

Bo kept searching.

Mom's ribbon bin fit all the marbles, but it was too big.

Uncle Ben's tool crate was smaller but not small enough.

Bo found a plastic vase the family used
to store their stickball sticks.

Would it hold all the marbles?

He carefully put them in.

Hawa! They fit. And they looked good.

Bo admired the marbles from all sides. Then he saw his favorite redbird marble at the bottom. The best one should be on top!

He started to take out the marbles . . .

but his arm was too short.

How could he sell the marbles
if he couldn't reach them?

Bo trudged out to the porch.
"Elisi, I can't find anything," he said.

"I'll help you in a minute,"
Grandma said. "Just keep looking."

"But I've looked *everywhere!*" wailed Bo.

"Everywhere?" Grandma asked. "Are you sure?"

Bo went back to his room and flopped onto the bed.

Think! There had to be something the right size.

Then he saw it.

His grandmother was always telling him to put away his things. She had even made him a special basket to hold his fossil collection.

It was shorter than the vase. And the bottom was smaller than the mat.

Would it hold all the marbles?

"Ni, Elisi!" he called. "This basket you made for me is just right!"

"Hawa," she agreed. "I knew you'd find something."

She looked around the room.
"And I'll still help you, like I promised . . .
I'll help you clean up this mess!"

The next day, Bo's marbles were a big success.
Everyone wanted to buy one.

"After all this work, we need to squeeze in some playtime,"
Uncle Ben told Bo. "And I think I know just the game."

Hawa!

Dikaneisdi ᎠᎢᏫᏘᎥᎦᏗ * Glossary
(dee-ka-NAYS-dee)

Atsutsa (ah-JOO-jah)	ᎠᏍᎦ	Boy or young man, often shortened to *chooch*		**Ni** (NEE)	Ꮒ	Look!
Elisi (eh-LEE-see)	ᎡᎵᏏ	My grandmother		**Osdadv** (ohs-DAH-dunh)	ᎣᏍᏓᏛ	Very good; excellent
Gado usdi (gah-do OOS-dee)	ᎦᏙ ᎤᏍᏗ	What? What is it?		**Tla** (KLAH)	Ꮭ	No; not
Hawa (ha-WAH)	ᎭᏩ	OK! All right!				

Cherokee marbles, digadayosdi or ᏗᎦᏓᏴᏍᏗ, is an ancient game still played today. Some players use traditional marbles chipped from stone and sanded smooth using a piece of sandstone and water. But most players use billiard balls.

Usually teams of three play on an L-shaped outdoor course with five holes about forty feet apart. The players throw their marbles toward each hole in order, playing up the course and back again. Players also try to knock their opponents' marbles away from the holes. The first team to complete the course wins.

Cherokee marbles is one of the traditional games played each year during the Cherokee National Holiday in Tahlequah, Oklahoma, capital of the Cherokee Nation of Oklahoma. More than one hundred thousand Cherokee people and other visitors come to town over the Labor Day weekend for traditional sporting events, such as stickball and chunkey; cooking contests; arts and crafts vendors; a powwow; and the annual State of the Nation speech from the principal chief.

Exploring the Math

Bo is proud of his stone marbles and wants to find just the right container to display them at the Cherokee National Holiday. It has to be big enough to hold all the marbles but small enough to fit on the table in his family's booth. As Bo searches for a solution, he discovers that containers of different shapes can hold the same amount.

Bo explores the math of volume, capacity, and area as he participates in an important community tradition. Hands-on learning like this helps children build math skills for school and daily life.

Try this!

* **Gather various plastic containers and help children measure and pour** a cup of water into each. Before pouring, encourage children to predict where the water line will fall.

* **Explore area by giving each person twelve identical square crackers** or sticky notes. Everyone uses their crackers to create a shape. (No overlaps!) Then compare creations.

* **Help children use tape and paper to make two cones:** one wide and short, one tall and thin. After children predict which cone will hold more, help them use uncooked rice or beans to find out.

* **Talk about containers around you.** "Will the soup in the big, wide pot fit in this tall, thin container?" "Let's see if all your toy unicorns can ride in your dump truck!"

Look for opportunities for children to help you fill backpacks, lunchboxes, and other containers. Maybe you can ask them for help the next time you pack up leftovers!

**—Dr. Sharon Nelson-Barber
(Rappahannock descent)**
Director, Culture & Language in STEM Education, WestEd

Visit www.charlesbridge.com/storytellingmath for more activities.

For Katie and Jesse: you teach me something new every day—A. C.

To my two beautiful grandmothers, Dean and Molly, who are two of the best teachers I've ever had—M. G.

This book is supported in part by TERC under a grant from the Heising-Simons Foundation.

At the time of publication, all URLs printed in this book were accurate and active. Charlesbridge, TERC, the author, and the illustrator are not responsible for the content or accessibility of any website.

Developed in conjunction with TERC
2067 Massachusetts Avenue
Cambridge, MA 02140
(617) 873-9600
www.terc.edu

Published by Charlesbridge
9 Galen Street
Watertown, MA 02472
(617) 926-0329
www.charlesbridge.com

Printed in China
(hc) 10 9 8 7 6 5 4 3 2 1
(pb) 10 9 8 7 6 5 4 3 2 1

Library of Congress Cataloging-in-Publication Data
Names: Coulson, Art, 1961– author. | Goodnight, Madelyn, illustrator.
Title: Look, Grandma! Ni, Elisi! / by Art Coulson; illustrated by Madelyn Goodnight.
Description: Watertown, MA: Charlesbridge Publishing, [2021] | Series: Storytelling math | Audience: Ages 3–6. | Audience: Grades K–1. | Summary: "Bo wants to find the perfect container to show off his traditional marbles for the Cherokee National Holiday in this exploration of volume and capacity." —Provided by publisher.
Identifiers: LCCN 2020017263 (print) | LCCN 2020017264 (ebook) | ISBN 9781623542030 (hardcover) | ISBN 9781623542047 (trade paperback) | ISBN 9781632899552 (ebook)
Subjects: CYAC: Marbles (Game objects)—Fiction. | Volume (Cubic content)—Fiction. | Cherokee Indians—Fiction. | Indians of North America—Oklahoma—Fiction.
Classification: LCC PZ7.1.C6758 Lo 2021 (print) | LCC PZ7.1.C6758 (ebook) | DDC [E]—dc23
LC record available at https://lccn.loc.gov/2020017263
LC ebook record available at https://lccn.loc.gov/2020017264

Illustrations done in digital media
Display type set in FF Bokka by John Critchley and Darren Raven
Text type set in Helenita Book by Rodrigo Araya Salas
Color separations by Colourscan Print Co Pte Ltd, Singapore
Printed by 1010 Printing International Limited in Huizhou, Guangdong, China
Production supervision by Jennifer Most Delaney
Designed by Jon Simeon